Billie B. Brown

Billie B. Brown Books

The Bad Butterfly
The Soccer Star
The Midnight Feast
The Second-best Friend
The Extra-special Helper
The Beautiful Haircut
The Big Sister
The Spotty Vacation
The Birthday Mix-up
The Secret Message
The Little Lie
The Best Project
The Deep End
The Copycat Kid
The Night Fright

First American Edition 2013
Kane Miller, A Division of EDC Publishing

Text Copyright © 2011 Sally Rippin
Illustrations Copyright © 2011 Aki Fukuoka
Logo and design copyright © 2010 Hardie Grant Egmont

First published in Australia as The Spotty Holiday in 2011
by Hardie Grant Egmont

For information contact:
Kane Miller, A Division of EDC Publishing
P.O. Box 470663
Tulsa, OK 74147-0663
www.kanemiller.com
www.edcpub.com
www.usbornebooksandmore.com

Library of Congress Control Number: 2012956110

Printed and bound in the United States of America
9 10 11 12 13 14 15 16 17 18
ISBN: 978-1-61067-183-5

The
Spotty
Vacation

By Sally Rippin

Illustrated by Aki Fukuoka

Kane Miller

A DIVISION OF EDC PUBLISHING

Chapter One

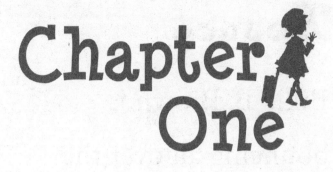

Billie B. Brown has
one package of mints,
twelve colored pencils
and a brand-new suitcase
on wheels. Do you know
what the "B" in Billie B.
Brown stands for?

Bouncy.

Billie B. Brown is bouncing all over the place. She is as excited as a bunny! Do you know why Billie is so excited? She's going to stay with her grandma for a whole week!

Billie loves her grandma.

One package
of mints

Twelve colored
pencils

A brand-new suitcase
on wheels

She lives in a city
that is very far away.
Too far away to drive.
So Grandma is taking
Billie there on a plane.
How exciting!

On the plane, Grandma
lets Billie sit by the
window. Billie has never
been on a plane before.

She wants to try all
the buttons and games.
She eats her whole
package of mints before
the plane even takes off.

"Billie," says her grandma. "How about you draw a picture or read a book?"

But Billie is too **excited** to draw or read. She has been counting sleeps for weeks!

When the plane takes off, it moves very fast and makes a loud noise. Billie is a teensy bit **scared**.

6

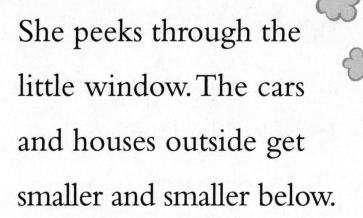

She peeks through the
little window. The cars
and houses outside get
smaller and smaller below.

Billie has never seen anything so wonderful. It looks like fairyland! She's not scared anymore. But she squeezes Grandma's hand as they go through the clouds. **Bumpity bump bump**.

Billie has written a list of all the fun things they are going to do at Grandma's.

Zoo

Shopping - new shoes (Purple ones?)

Movies

Adventure Playground

~~Waterworld~~ (no Waterworld near

Grandma's house)

Billie can't *wait* until they get there. They have so much to do!

Chapter Two

When they arrive at
Grandma's apartment it
is already dark.

Billie feels very tired.
Grandma tucks Billie into
a sofa bed in the study.

The sheets feel cool and crisp. But Billie feels **hot** and **itchy**. She has a bit of a tummy ache.

"Probably just all the excitement, love," Grandma says. She kisses Billie good night. "You'll feel better tomorrow."

Billie finds it very hard to get to sleep.

Grandma's apartment
looks spooky in the dark.
The traffic outside is
very noisy! And Billie
feels hotter and itchier
than ever.

When Billie wakes
up the next morning
she is covered in spots.
Do you know what
they are? Chickenpox!

"Chickenpox?" says Billie.

"Chickenpox," says
Grandma, shaking her
head. "Luckily I've already
had it so I can't catch
it again.

But we don't want
other children catching it.
You'll have to stay inside
until you are better."

"But what about the
zoo?" Billie gasps. "And
the movies? And my new
shoes?"

Big fat tears roll down Billie's spotty cheeks.

"I'm sorry," sighs Grandma. "But there's nothing we can do. How about you get out your sketchbook and pencils? I'll make you breakfast in bed. French toast?"

"With banana?" Billie says, wiping her eyes.

"With banana," says Grandma.

Billie eats up all her breakfast. Then she calls her mom and dad.

"Guess what?" Billie's mom says. "Baby Noah has chickenpox, too!"

Billie laughs. She can't imagine her little brother all covered in spots.

"Hello, Noah!" Billie
shouts down the phone.

After Billie says goodbye,
she climbs back into
bed and takes out her
sketchbook and pencils.

But it's no use. She can't think of anything to draw.

Billie feels **itchy** and **scratchy** all over. Grandma says that Billie shouldn't scratch her spots or they will scar. Billie sighs. She wishes she could go outside to the park and the shops and the zoo.

18

Billie wrote so many fun things on her list and now she can't do any of them. What a miserable vacation!

Then, Billie has an idea. A super-duper idea!

You'll never guess what she is up to.

Chapter Three

"OK, Grandma," Billie calls.
"You can come in now!"

Grandma walks into
the family room.
"Wow, Billie! This looks
amazing," she says.

Billie giggles. Grandma
is right. The family room
looks…well, it doesn't
look like a family room
anymore.

Billie has been drawing
pictures of zoo animals all
morning. While Grandma
made lunch, Billie stuck
the pictures around
the room.

She even moved some
of Grandma's furniture
to look like cages.
Now the family room
looks like a zoo!

Grandma and Billie
walk around Billie's zoo
looking at all the animals.
"Be careful of that one!"
Billie says. She points to
Mr. Fred who is sitting in
Grandma's laundry basket.
"He's a ferocious bear!"

Grandma pretends
to look scared.
Billie laughs.

Grandma has packed
a picnic for lunch.
After they have seen
all the animals, they sit
down on the carpet to
eat their sandwiches.

"How about we go to the ice cream shop next?"asks Grandma, winking.

"Yay!" says Billie following Grandma into the kitchen.

Grandma pretends to be the ice cream shop lady. She hands Billie a bowl of vanilla ice cream. Billie hands her some pretend money.

Then Grandma takes some things out of the cupboard. Bananas, chocolate chips, peanut butter, maple syrup and sprinkles.

"Would you like to choose a topping, madam?" she asks in a silly voice.

"Can I put anything on it?" Billie asks.

"Of course!" says Grandma.

Billie smiles. "Can I put *everything* on it?"

Grandma laughs. "Whatever you like, love."

Billie mixes everything into her ice cream until it is a big, goopy mess. Delicious! This vacation is much more fun than she thought.

That night after Billie's
bath, Grandma puts a
special cream on Billie's
spots to stop them itching.

The spots are red and even itchier than before. But Billie is doing a very good job of not scratching them.

When Grandma has finished, Billie hops into bed and takes out her vacation list. She crosses out Zoo. What is next?

Shopping - new shoes.

Oh dear! How can
they go shoe shopping
when Billie has to
stay inside? But then
Billie has another idea.
A super-duper idea.
Even super-duperer
than the last one!

Can you guess what
she is thinking?

Chapter Four

The next morning Billie gets up early. There is so much to do!

"What's our plan for today?" Grandma asks over breakfast.

"Shoe shopping!" says Billie.

"Great," says Grandma. "I love shopping for shoes!"

Billie and Grandma go into Grandma's bedroom. Billie tries on all the shoes in the closet. Pink ones, sparkly ones, boots and sandals.

Finally Billie finds the
perfect shoes. They are
exactly the same purple
as Billie's T-shirt. They are
a teensy bit big, but Billie
doesn't mind.

Billie and Grandma
pay Mr. Fred, who is
the shopkeeper.

Billie crosses Shopping -
new shoes off her list.

"What's next?" asks
Grandma.

"Going to the movies,"
says Billie.

"Hmm, OK," says Grandma.

"How about I ask my neighbor to pick us up some DVDs? We can make popcorn!"

"Yay!" says Billie. She jumps up and down in **excitement**.

"Glad to see you're still my bouncy Billie," says Grandma. "Even with the chickenpox!"

Billie makes movie
tickets for herself and
Grandma. Then she
closes all the blinds in
the family room so it is
nice and dark. Just like
at the movies!

When the theater is
ready, she helps Grandma
make popcorn in a big
pan.

Billie loves watching the popcorn jump around inside the pan. **Pop pop pop!**

Billie and Grandma spend all week inside, but Billie never gets bored.

One morning Billie makes an adventure playground out of cushions. And that night she gets to play Waterworld – in the bathtub. What a mess!

On the last day of her vacation, Billie's spots have cleared up enough for her to go outside.

Which is lucky because it is time for Billie and Grandma to catch the plane home again.

On the plane, Billie fiddles with all the buttons on the armrest. She accidentally pushes the button to call the flight attendant.

"Oops, sorry!" says Billie when the woman arrives.

"That's all right, dear,"
says the attendant.
She smiles at Billie
and Grandma. "Are you
on vacation with your
grandma?"

"Yes," says Billie. "But I
got the chickenpox so
I couldn't go outside.
We had to stay inside
for a whole week!"

"Oh, what a shame," says the attendant. "That must have been a pretty boring vacation."

"No way," says Billie.

"We went to the zoo and ate ice cream. We went shopping and I even went to Waterworld!"

"Waterworld?" says the attendant. "But I thought you stayed at home?"

"We did," says Billie. "And I had the best vacation ever!"

The flight attendant looks confused.

But Billie and Grandma
look at each other
and giggle.

Collect them all!

Billie B. Brown
The Bad Butterfly
By Sally Rippin

Billie B. Brown
The Soccer Star
By Sally Rippin

Billie B. Brown
The Second-best Friend
By Sally Rippin

Billie B. Brown
The Midnight Feast
By Sally Rippin

Billie B. Brown
The Beautiful Haircut
By Sally Rippin

Billie B. Brown
The Extra-special Helper
By Sally Rippin

Billie B. Brown
The Big Sister
By Sally Rippin

Billie B. Brown
The Birthday Mix-up
By Sally Rippin

Billie B. Brown
The Spotty Vacation
By Sally Rippin

Play cool games
and visit Billie at
www.BillieBBrownBooks.com